Gang of Fire

Jonny Zucker

Illustrated by
Paul Savage

Titles in Full Flight 2

Badger Publishing Limited
26 Wedgwood Way, Pin Green Industrial Estate, Stevenage,
Hertfordshire SG1 4QF
Telephone: 01438 356907. Fax: 01438 747015.
www.badger-publishing.co.uk enquiries@badger-publishing.co.uk

Gang of Fire ISBN 1 85880 371 3

Series Editor: Jonny Zucker
Publisher: David Jamieson
Editor: Paul Martin
Design: Jain Birchenough
Cover illustration: Paul Savage
Printed and bound in China through Colorcraft Ltd., Hong Kong

Gang of Fire

Jonny Zucker

Contents

Badger Publishing

Chapter 1 - Fire

Paul hadn't really wanted to join Howie's gang.

His best mate Nat had told him to steer well clear.

"Howie's trouble," Nat warned him. "It's not worth it."

But Howie had been on at Paul for weeks.

Howie who ruled the playground with his bunch of cronies.

Howie with his razor-sharp stares.

Howie the loud mouth, whose
favourite line was 'Who's scared now?'

On their way home from school one
day, Paul told Nat.

"I'm joining up," he said as they walked
down the high street. "I've got three tasks
to do if I want to make it into the gang."

"You're joking, right?" asked Nat.

But Paul was already running across the road towards a phone box.

He disappeared inside.

Seconds later Paul ran out of the phone box towards Nat, shouting "RUN!"

Nat didn't need to be told twice.

He started to leg it with Paul. He looked back to catch the sight of smoke drifting up out of the phone box.

As he and Paul raced to the corner of the high street, they spied Howie leaning on a wall outside the paint shop.

He had seen everything.

And he was laughing.

Chapter 2 - Broken Glass

That evening, Nat phoned Paul.

"What the hell was that about?"
he asked.

"The phone box?" replied Paul.

"You know what I mean," Nat hissed.

"That was task one for joining the
gang," Paul said.

"Are you crazy?" Nat asked.

There was silence for a few seconds
and then Paul spoke again.

"It's just something I've got to do."

"No you don't," Nat said angrily. "Tell Howie to find some other mug for his gang."

But Paul wasn't listening.

"Got to go mate," he said. "Howie and the lads are waiting for me outside."

Over the next few days at school, Paul avoided Nat whenever he could. Nat tried to talk to him, but Paul was always in a hurry. Always in a hurry to meet up with Howie.

Nat and Paul normally hung out on Saturdays but that weekend Nat heard nothing from Paul.

At one a.m. on Sunday morning, Nat was woken by the sound of glass breaking in the street outside.

He leapt out of bed and sprang quickly towards the window. He pulled the curtain back. A group of five lads were running away from Mr Bentley's car next door.

The glass of the passenger door window had been smashed in.

As they darted off through the shadows, one of them looked back at the car.

In the dim light, Nat could swear he knew the face.

It was Paul.

Chapter 3 - Check Out

There were three loud knocks on Nat's front door.

Nat's mum went to open it.

There were two policemen on the doorstep.

Nat's mum let them in.

They wanted to know if anyone had heard anything in the night.

Mr Bentley's car stereo had been nicked. The police thought it had been taken by a group of local youths.

Nat's mum, dad and little sister, Angie, looked blank.

"What about you?" asked one of the policemen, turning to Nat.

Nat shook his head.

"I don't know anything about a car stereo," he answered.

The policemen left and Angie gave Nat a funny look.

Later that afternoon Paul turned up at Nat's.

"What do you want?" asked Nat.
"You've hardly spoken to me all week."

"Can I come in?" Paul asked.

"S'pose so" replied Nat.

They went to Nat's room

"Look what I've got," grinned Paul, reaching into his bag. He pulled out a car stereo.

"Have you lost the plot?" Nat blurted out.

"I had to do it," Paul said firmly.
"It was the second task for the gang."

"The police were round here this morning," said Nat, "asking if we'd heard anything from next door."

For a minute Paul looked worried.

"And did anyone?" he asked.

"No," replied Nat, "but that's not the point."

"Of course it's the point," smiled Paul.

"They'll never know it was me. I was wearing gloves, they'll be no fingerprints or anything."

Suddenly, they heard a noise by Nat's bedroom door. Nat quickly reached the door and yanked it open. Angie was standing outside. She'd been listening to them.

Paul grabbed Angie by the arm and pulled her inside the room. He slammed the door.

"I don't know how much you heard," he snarled at her, "but you're to keep your mouth shut. Do you get me?"

Angie nodded.

"Leave her alone," Nat shouted, moving towards Paul.

Paul let go of Angie.

He scowled at Nat and threw the stereo back into his bag.

"See you later," he hissed.

And then he was gone.

Chapter 4 - Tempers Fly

On Monday morning Nat saw Paul by the school bike sheds.

"Look Paul, this has gone too far," he began. "Howie's full of hot air. He gets gang members to do strikes whilst he just looks on and does nothing. The only thing you'll get from being in his gang is hassle."

Paul was about to answer, but Nat felt an arm round his neck.

He was pinned against a wall.

"Who's scared now?" laughed Howie as one of his gang, a boy called Keith, held Nat.

"I know what your game is," said Howie smiling. An evil smile.

"You're trying to talk Paul out of the gang, aren't you?"

Nat stared Howie out.

"And anyway, who are you?" said Howie. "You're just some scared little rat. And I can tell you something for free. You'll never be asked to join my gang."

Nat freed himself from Keith's grip.

"I wouldn't join your pathetic gang even if you begged me."

Nat spat out the words.

"Leave the little rat alone," mocked Howie.

Howie and Keith started to walk away.

Paul looked at Nat for a second and then turned and ran to catch up with Howie.

Chapter 5 - Phone Rage

"It's me."

Nat held the phone for a few seconds before replying.

"Why are you phoning me, Paul?"

"It's about what happened by the bike sheds. Howie was out of order."

"Didn't see you stepping in," muttered Nat.

"I just thought I'd let you know that my third task is on for Sunday."

"What is it this time?" Nat asked, not really wanting to hear the answer.

"I'm spraying the gang's tag line across the railway bridge at 2.

"Howie and the rest of the gang will be there to watch."

Nat raised his voice. "No way Paul. Pull out. I've never heard of anything more stupid.

"Can't you see Howie's game? You'll do the tag line and Howie will get all the credit. And anyway the tracks are electrified and there are hundred mile an hour trains down there all the time."

Paul snapped back quickly.

"You know what, maybe Howie was right. You are just a scared little rat. I'm doing it and that's that."

Paul slammed down the phone.

Chapter 6 - The Railway Bridge

"You OK to look after Angie for a couple of hours?"

Nat was lying on the sofa watching a football programme.

His mum stood between Nat and the TV.

He nodded.

"Yeah, that's OK," he answered without looking up.

"Me and dad need to do a bit of shopping," Nat's mum informed him. She went off to get his dad.

Nat glanced at his watch. 1.45 p.m. Sunday afternoon.

He suddenly sat bolt upright.

He heard the door shut behind his parents.

"Angie, get your coat," he yelled.

"Why?" she asked, walking in from her room. "Where are we going?"

"You'll see when we get there," he replied sharply.

He grabbed her hand and hurried out of the flat.

They ran down the street and cut through the alley and across the estate. Five minutes later they'd reached the fence by the side of the railway.

Nat found a small hole in the fence and looked through.

"What are you looking at?" Angie demanded.

"I'll let you have a go in a minute," Nat told her.

He looked at the scene taking place on the other side of the track. There was Paul - a can in his right hand, spraying Howie's tag line across the underside of the bridge in huge blue strokes.

Howie and the rest of his gang were there too. Watching. And loving it.

"Here, have a look," Nat told Angie.

She stood on tiptoe to look through the hole. "I can't believe it," she whispered.

After a minute she stood down and let Nat have his place back by the hole. Nat looked on as Paul continued to spray the bridge.

Without any warning, Angie moved away from Nat

She crept along the pavement and found a much bigger hole in the fence.

She slipped through and started running down the bank towards the railway track, shouting at Paul and the gang not to be so stupid.

"You're ruining the bridge!" she yelled.

Nat watched in horror as she made it down to the track.

She carried on calling out to Paul and the rest of them for a few seconds but then she screamed in pain. She seemed to have got her foot caught in one of the tracks.

Suddenly the roar of an approaching train sounded in the distance.

Paul, Howie and the rest of the gang stood frozen to the spot, fear dotted all over their faces.

Chapter 7 - Off The Tracks

Nat didn't wait.

He was off and through the hole in seconds.

He scrambled down the bank as the sound of the train got louder and louder.

Angie was screaming.

Nat dived towards the track.

He could now see the train. It was coming at an incredible speed.

Paul, Howie and the gang were still standing there, not moving, gripped by terror.

The train driver must have seen Angie because the train's horn was roaring at full blast.

Nat moved as quickly as he could, but the train was pounding straight towards Angie.

He made a lunge for his sister and dragged her off the line a second before the train crashed past.

The train sped on and disappeared after a few moments.

Angie clung onto Nat and sobbed.

"My ankle hurts," she groaned.

Paul threw down the spray can in disgust and started to cross the track towards Nat and Angie.

"I've been a complete idiot and a bad friend," Paul called as he approached them, his face full of shame.

"It doesn't matter," replied Nat, as he tried to calm Angie down.

"It does matter. You were right about Howie," Paul said.

"He's just a bully who gets other kids to do his dirty work. I'm out of his gang. It's a complete waste of time. I'll leave Mr Bentley's stereo on his doorstep. I'll even leave him some money for the broken car window."

Angie stopped crying.

"I'll help you to pay back Mr Bentley's money," she said, wiping her eyes.

"Thanks, but it's up to me to sort it," smiled Paul.

Paul, Nat and Angie looked back across the tracks at Howie and his gang. They were still standing there rooted to the spot.

And they still looked scared to death.

"Come on, let's go home" said Nat quietly.

They began to walk away, with Angie hobbling.

But Paul turned back and stared long and hard at Howie.

Across the track he mouthed slowly and very carefully, "Who's scared now?"